56 51 56 57 42 44 44 45 46

107 108 109 110 111 1 11

308 309 310 311 312 313 314 31

591 592 593 594 595 596 597 598

691 692 693 694 695 696 697 69

791 792 793 794 795 796 797 798

891 892 893 894 895 896 897 898

991 992 993 994 995 996 997 998

1085 1086 1087 1088 1089 10 901

1471 147 214 731 47 414 75 147

126 310 831 622 59 833 361 108

958 601 783 062 810 966 722 269 88

21 061 243 126 866 268 011 663 19

803 310 038 608 976 863 106 708

167 832 081 876 306 787 317 87

891 368 216 610 808 831 062 810

608

591 891 818 260 361 012 685 936

691 600 685 268 876 126 866

INFINITY
and Me

written by
Kate Hosford

illustrations by
Gabi Swiątkowska

CAROLRHODA BOOKS • MINNEAPOLIS

Thank you to my sons and the other children who inspired me with their thoughts about infinity. Thanks also to Jean Pugni and Andreas Welch for the circular music, editor Anna Cavallo for her insight and support, Uma Krishnaswami for her expertise, and my friend and collaborator, Gabi Swiatkowska, for her beautiful illustrations. —K.H.

Carolrhoda Books
A division of Lerner Publishing Group, Inc.
241 First Avenue North
Minneapolis, MN 55401 U.S.A.

Website address: www.lernerbooks.com

Main body text set in Venis Pro Medium 16/24.
Typeface provided by the Chank Company.

Library of Congress Cataloging-in-Publication Data

Hosford, Kate.
    Infinity and me / by Kate Hosford ; illustrated by Gabi Swiatkowska.
        p.   cm.
    Summary: After the sight of a night sky filled with stars makes eight-year-old Uma feel very small, she asks people how they think about infinity and gets a variety of answers before realizing the comfort in knowing that some things go on forever.
    ISBN: 978-0-7613-6726-0 (lib. bdg. : alk. paper)
    [1. Infinity—Fiction. 2. Grandmothers—Fiction. 3. Schools—Fiction.]
I. Swiatkowska, Gabi, ill. II. Title.
PZ7.H79313Inf 2012
[E]—dc23   2011044746

Manufactured in the United States of America
1 - DP - 7/15/12

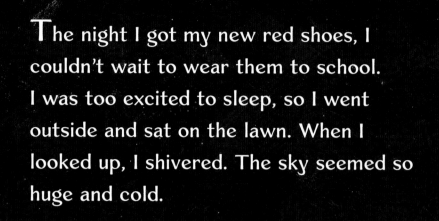

The night I got my new red shoes, I
couldn't wait to wear them to school.
I was too excited to sleep, so I went
outside and sat on the lawn. When I
looked up, I shivered. The sky seemed so
huge and cold.

How many stars were in the sky?
A million? A billion?
Maybe the number was as
big as infinity.

I started to feel very,
very small. How
could I even think
about something as
big as infinity?

At school the next day, I asked
my friend Charlie how he
imagines **infinity**.
"That's easy, Uma." he said.

"It's a giant number that keeps **growing bigger and bigger forever.**"

I thought about trying to write that number down. Even if I lived forever, I would never finish.

I went to get ice cream after school with my best friend, Samantha. "Sam," I asked her, "when you think about infinity, what do you see?"

"I see the infinity symbol," she said. "It looks kind of like an eight that fell over and took a nap. If it were a racetrack, I could drive around it forever."

Samantha made me feel a little better. Writing that symbol wouldn't take long at all. I traced a napping eight in the dirt with my shoe.

Before school the next day, I asked Grandma
how she imagines infinity. She smiled at
me and said, "I like to think about a family.
First, you have the great grandparents,
then the grandparents, parents, children,
grandchildren, and great grandchildren . . .
It could go on forever."

I couldn't really imagine that
many people in one family.
But I did realize something. It
was hard to talk about infinity
without talking about "forever."
I also realized something else.

Not one person had
noticed my new red shoes.
Not even Grandma, who
usually notices everything.
I looked down to make
sure they were still shiny.

Then I started to
wonder, what would I
like to do forever?

At first, I thought that I might
like to have recess forever.

But if there's no school before
recess, and no school after recess,

is it really
recess anymore?

Maybe I'd like to be eight forever,

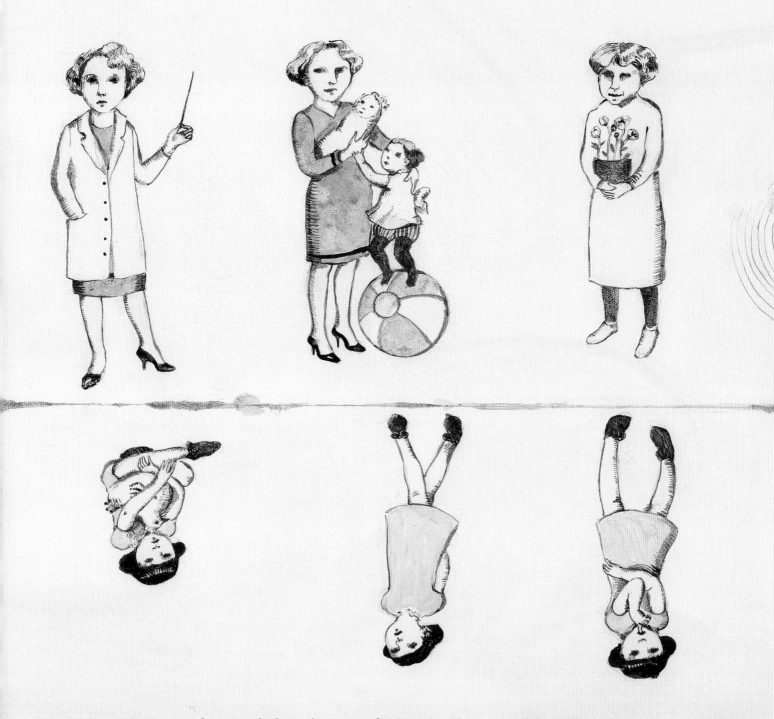

but I didn't know if Samantha would still
want to be my best friend when she was
eighty-five and I was still eight.

Maybe I could lick an ice-cream
cone forever, but what if my tongue
started to hurt?

Actually, my
head was
starting to
hurt from
all these
thoughts.

When I went to the lunchroom,
I asked our cook, Mr. Mancini,
how he imagines infinity.

He held up a
noodle. "How
many times do
you think you
could cut this in
half?" he asked.

I cut it in half six times, but then
it got too small and I was afraid I
might cut my finger instead of the
noodle. "In your mind," Mr. Mancini
said, "could you cut that tiny piece of
noodle in half forever?"

I asked Ms. Reed, our music teacher, about infinity and wished I hadn't. "Picture music that goes in a circle," she said. "The notes would lead us around and around. The music would be endless!"

I was starting to think
that my questions about
infinity might be endless.
It was time for me and
my red shoes to go home.

For dinner, Grandma made
my favorite meal, butter
chicken and rice. As she
mixed the spices, she
looked at me and said,

"Uma, I meant to tell you this morning—those are the most beautiful shoes I have ever seen!"

I didn't hear the rest of
what Grandma said. I was
too busy smiling. Right then
I knew—my love for her
was as big as infinity.

That night, I asked her if she would like to look at the stars with me. Snuggled up next to Grandma, the sky didn't seem so huge and cold anymore. Now it was more like a sparkly blanket, covering us both.

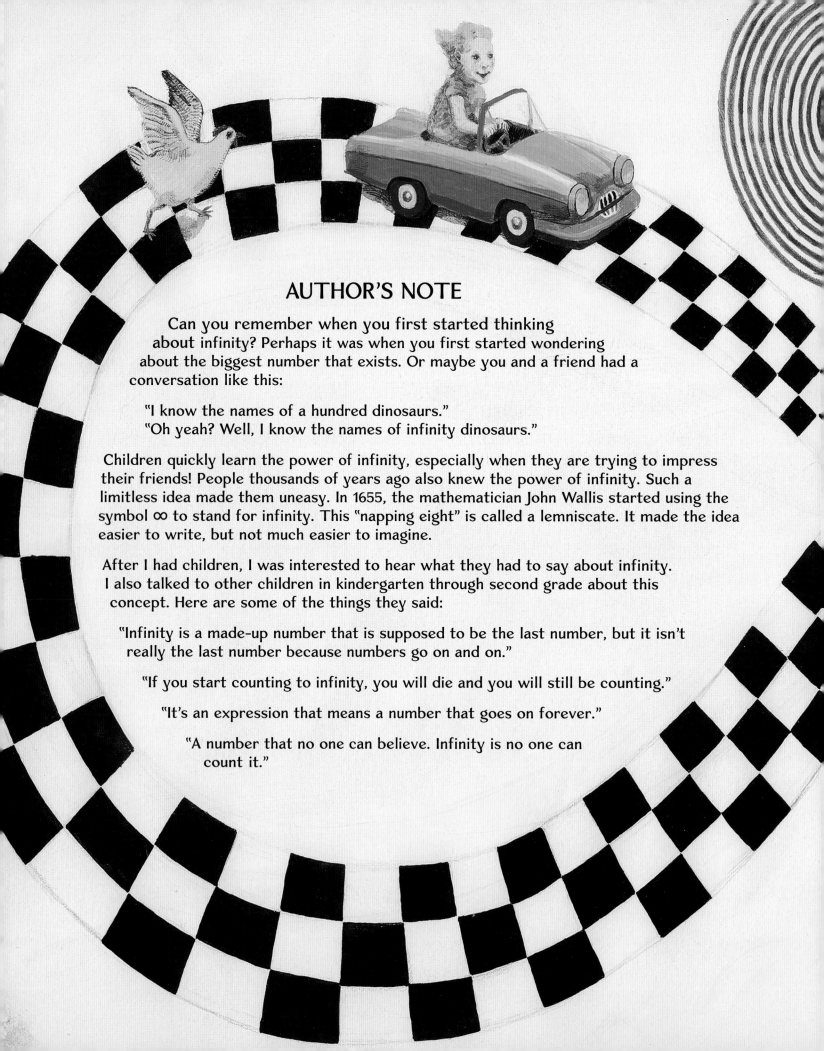

AUTHOR'S NOTE

Can you remember when you first started thinking
about infinity? Perhaps it was when you first started wondering
about the biggest number that exists. Or maybe you and a friend had a
conversation like this:

"I know the names of a hundred dinosaurs."
"Oh yeah? Well, I know the names of infinity dinosaurs."

Children quickly learn the power of infinity, especially when they are trying to impress
their friends! People thousands of years ago also knew the power of infinity. Such a
limitless idea made them uneasy. In 1655, the mathematician John Wallis started using the
symbol ∞ to stand for infinity. This "napping eight" is called a lemniscate. It made the idea
easier to write, but not much easier to imagine.

After I had children, I was interested to hear what they had to say about infinity.
I also talked to other children in kindergarten through second grade about this
concept. Here are some of the things they said:

"Infinity is a made-up number that is supposed to be the last number, but it isn't
really the last number because numbers go on and on."

"If you start counting to infinity, you will die and you will still be counting."

"It's an expression that means a number that goes on forever."

"A number that no one can believe. Infinity is no one can
count it."

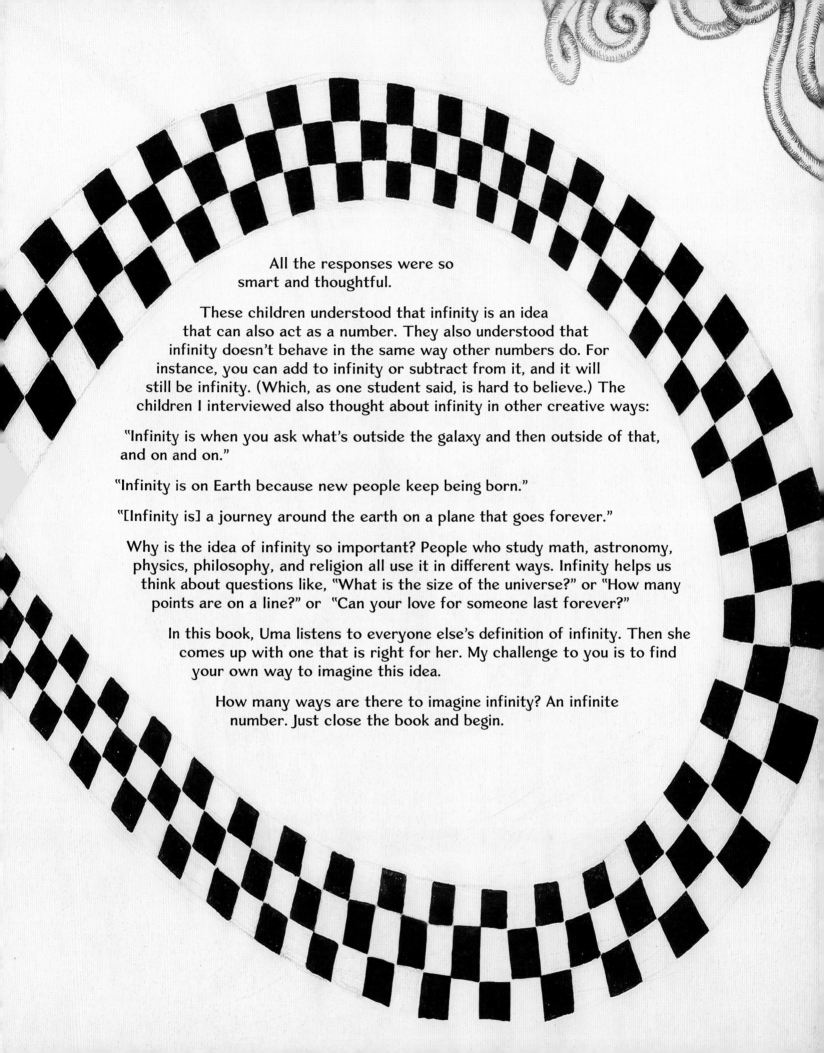

All the responses were so
smart and thoughtful.

These children understood that infinity is an idea
that can also act as a number. They also understood that
infinity doesn't behave in the same way other numbers do. For
instance, you can add to infinity or subtract from it, and it will
still be infinity. (Which, as one student said, is hard to believe.) The
children I interviewed also thought about infinity in other creative ways:

"Infinity is when you ask what's outside the galaxy and then outside of that,
and on and on."

"Infinity is on Earth because new people keep being born."

"[Infinity is] a journey around the earth on a plane that goes forever."

Why is the idea of infinity so important? People who study math, astronomy,
physics, philosophy, and religion all use it in different ways. Infinity helps us
think about questions like, "What is the size of the universe?" or "How many
points are on a line?" or "Can your love for someone last forever?"

In this book, Uma listens to everyone else's definition of infinity. Then she
comes up with one that is right for her. My challenge to you is to find
your own way to imagine this idea.

How many ways are there to imagine infinity? An infinite
number. Just close the book and begin.